Adapted by **Bill Scollon**

Based on the episode written by **Ashley Mendoza**

Illustrated by **Loter, Inc.**

D🅘SNEP PRESS

Los Angeles • New York

Tonight is Story Night. Mickey is going to read a bedtime story.

"**Aw, shucks,**" says Goofy. "I thought it was Magic Night."

"How will we decide which story to read?" Minnie asks.

"I'll use magic to pick a book," says Goofy. "Book-a-doodle-doo. Fly away and shoo!"

Oh, no! Goofy uses the wrong magic words. All the stories disappear!

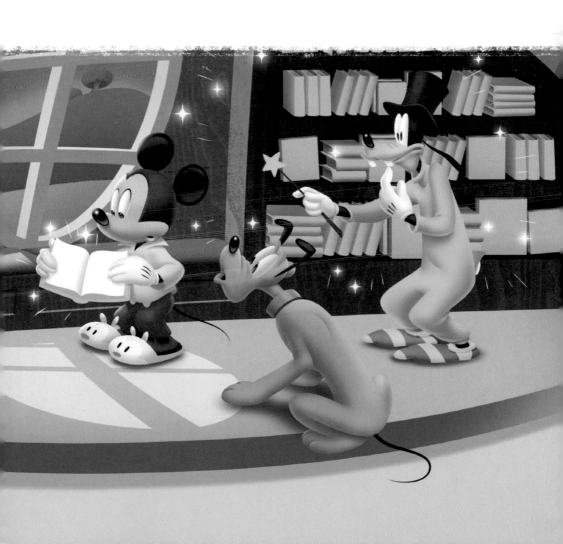

Mickey asks Professor Von Drake if he knows where the stories went.

"They're in a gold storybook in the Land of Fairy Tales," says the professor.

Outside, the professor opens a magic door to the Land of Fairy Tales.

"The gold storybook is in the Castle of the Beast," he says. "It has three shapes on its cover—a heart, a diamond, and a rose."

Oops! Goofy slips and falls through the magic door. A wall of glass slams shut!

"Hoo-boy," says the professor. "My remote control went kaput. Goofy's stuck."

"Oh, dear," Daisy says. "Goofy can't get the gold storybook by himself."

"He'll just goof up," adds Donald.

"I'm sure you can do it, pal," Mickey tells Goofy. "Good luck!"

Dressed in his new fairy-tale clothes, Goofy starts down
a path.

"**Gawrsh,**" says Goofy. "Which way leads to the
beast's castle?"

"Go right!" answers someone with a tiny voice.

Goofy is so surprised he falls to the ground.
"You're a goofy fella!" says a small knight.
"Goofyfella!" laughs Goofy. "That'll be my fairy-tale name."

"We're Chip and Dale Thumb," Chip, the small knight, says.
"But we've got to go," adds Dale Thumb. "Big problem at the castle!"
"Okay," says Goofyfella. "See ya!"

Soon Goofyfella comes upon Pied Piper Donald and Pluto the Merry Dog. They're trying to lead ducklings to a pond. "They won't follow me!" says Pied Piper Donald.

Goofyfella tries to teach Pied Piper Donald a new song. But he drops the flute, and it breaks.

"Sorry," he says. **"Oh, Toodles!"**

Toodles's cousin, Goofles, comes to help with four Mouseketools—suction cups, sticky tape, an oar, and a Mystery Mouseketool. Goofyfella chooses the tape to fix the flute. **It works!**

When Pied Piper Donald plays the new song, the ducklings line up and follow him. "Thanks!" he says.

"You're welcome," says Goofyfella. "How do I get to the castle?"

"Just go through the woods," Pied Piper Donald replies.

Deep in the woods, Goofyfella gets lost and runs into Hansel and Gretel Mouse. They're lost, too.

"Maybe somebody in that house can help us," says Goofyfella.

"No," Gretel Mouse warns. "That's the witch's house!"

Just then, someone calls, "Hello-o-o!" It's Witch Clarabelle

"Are you a good witch?" asks Goofyfella.

"Oh, yes," says Witch Clarabelle, laughing.

"I'm not scary at all."

Witch Clarabelle is making a big batch of Merry Muffins, but she can't find her mixing spoon.

Goofyfella calls for Goofles and chooses the oar. **"It's moo-arvelous!"** says Witch Clarabelle.

"I like being helpful," says Goofyfella. "But I need to get to the castle."

"Just follow the diamond shapes," says Witch Clarabelle.

The diamond shapes lead Goofyfella to a hill made of crystal.

The hill is super slippery. "**Whoopsie!** Looks like I need a Mouseketool," says Goofyfella.

"Oh, Goofles!"

Goofles has two Mouseketools left—the suction cups and the Mystery Mouseketool.

Goofyfella chooses the suction cups! He puts them on his shoes and marches right up the hill.

Goofyfella sees Chip and Dale Thumb at the castle door.

"We've come to rescue Daisy Beauty," Dale Thumb tells him.

"But we're so small," says Chip Thumb, "the beast can't hear us knocking."

"I'll just ring this bell," Goofyfella says. But he pulls on the rope too hard!

Beast Pete comes to the door. "What do you want?" he roars.

"We want you to let Daisy Beauty go!" says Chip Thumb.

"It's not nice to keep her locked inside," says Goofyfella.

"I know," Beast Pete admits. "I just wanted a friend."

"Well, let's have a party," Goofyfella says. "That's a good way to make friends."

Beast Pete is delighted. "Will you be my guest?" he politely asks Daisy Beauty.

Daisy Beauty sees that Beast Pete is really very kind.
"Yes," she answers. "We can be friends, too."
All of a sudden, Beast Pete turns into a prince. Daisy Beauty's friendship broke the spell!

Everyone enjoys the party—especially Prince Pete!

"I owe this all to you, Goofyfella," he says. "How can I repay you?"

"I'm looking for the gold storybook," Goofyfella says.

"If the book is in my library," says Prince Pete, "it's yours."

Prince Pete's library is stacked high with books.

"What does the gold storybook look like?"
he asks.

"It's decorated with a heart, a diamond,
and a rose," says Goofyfella.

"I see it!" shouts Daisy Beauty. "But it's up so high."

"I know just what to do," says Goofyfella.

"Oh, Goofles!"

The Mystery Mouseketool is a bunch of balloons! Goofyfella holds on to them and floats up to the top shelf. Then he grabs the gold storybook.

"I've got it!" shouts Goofyfella. "But how am I going to get down?"

Chip and Dale Thumb come to the rescue, popping the balloons one at a time.

Goofyfella safely drifts back to the ground.

At the Clubhouse, the professor gets the remote control working. He presses the button and the glass door opens. Goofy jumps right through.

"Goofy!" yells Mickey. **"You did it!"**